D0432947

No
Buddy
Like
a
Book

No Buddy Like a Book

Allan Wolf

illustrated by Brianne Farley

WALKER BOOKS
AND SUBSIDIARIES
LONDON • BOSTON • SYDNEY • AUCKLAND

"port"
"starboard"

WE learn important stuff from books.
We learn to speak and think.

We learn why icebergs stay afloat …
and why *Titanic*s sink.

We learn to play harmonica.
We learn to bake and cook.
We learn to read and write.
There is no buddy like a book.

wind
Around

But books are only smears of ink
without the reader's mind
to give the letters meaning
and to read between the lines.

BOOK
EXPRESS

So step aboard the Book Express.
It's waiting at the station.
But can you guess the address
of your final destination?

The greatest nation in the world:

your own imagination!

I've learnt to name the planets
and to track a distant star.
I've learnt to bottle moonlight
and to calculate how far

a solid rocket booster sends
a shuttle into space.
I've learnt to build a telescope
to see space face-to-face.

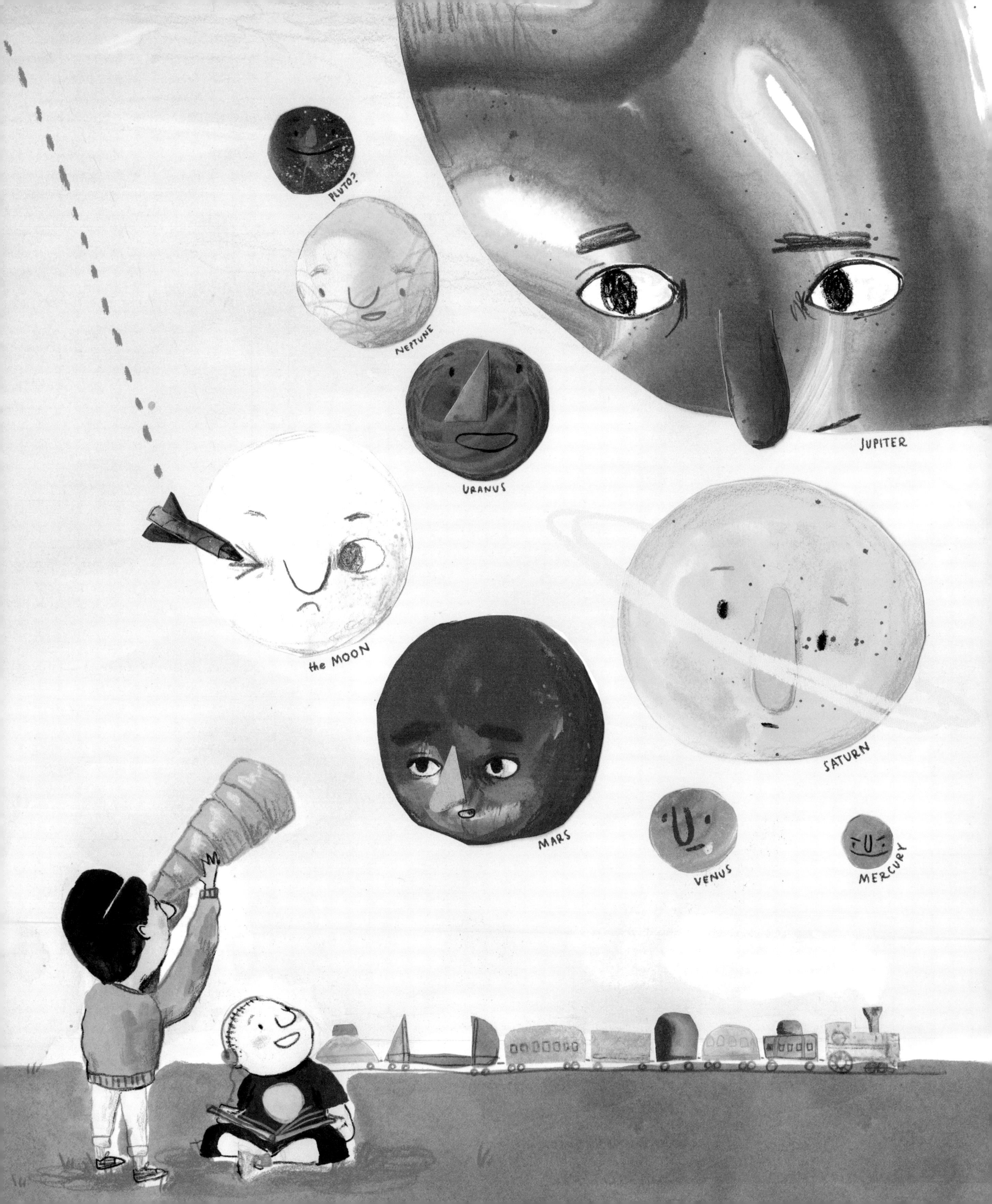
PLUTO?
NEPTUNE
URANUS
JUPITER
the MOON
SATURN
MARS
VENUS
MERCURY

This homemade pinhole camera
even lets me see the sun.
There is no buddy like a book
to show you how it's done.

1.

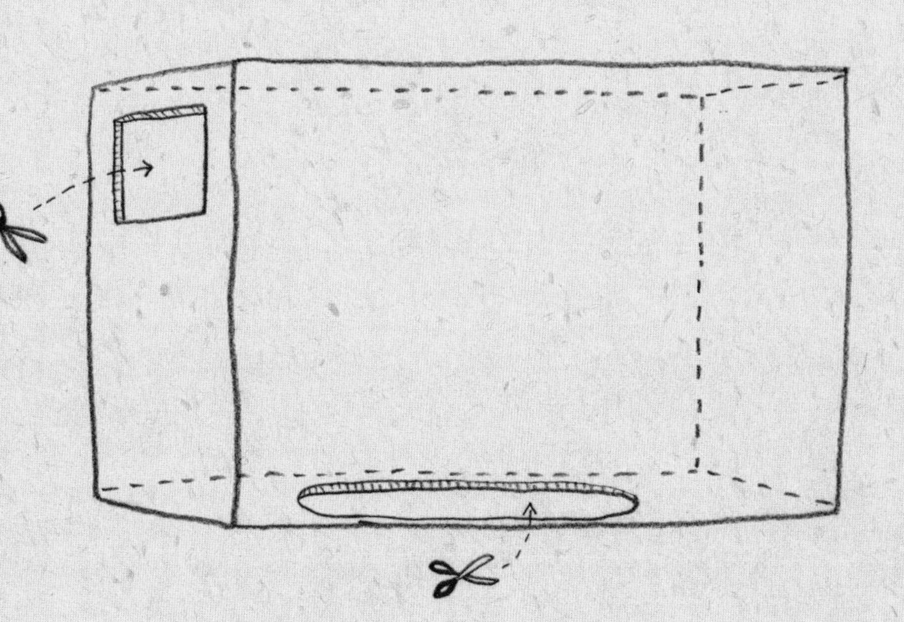

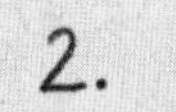

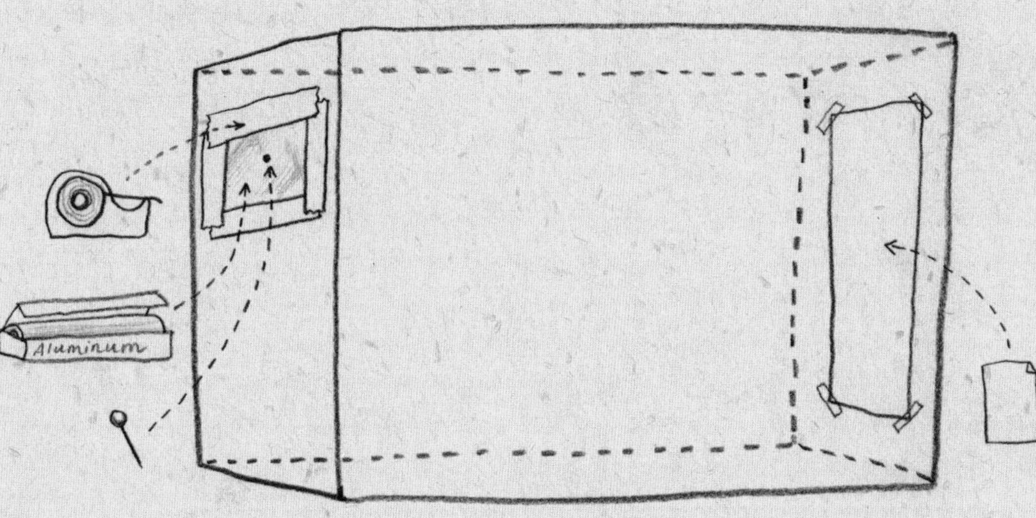

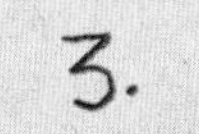

My launch pad is a science book.
My mind's a constellation.
The only rocket fuel I need
is my own imagination.

I hiked the Himalayas,
a strong wind at my back.
I've seen the sights of India
from high atop a yak.

I've anteloped in Africa
and kissed a crocodile
as I was sailing all alone
along the River Nile.

I'm quite the global traveller.
I've been to every land:
China, Thailand, Russia, Rome,
New Guinea and Sudan.

New Zealand and Australia,
Perth and Puerto Rico.
Canada and Kathmandu,
Liverpool and Glasgow.

SCARLET MACAW
HONDURAS
RAGGIANA
BIRD-OF-PARADISE
PAPUA NEW GUINEA
MOCKINGBIRD
UNITED STATES
SPINDALIS
PUERTO RICO
SPARROW
ITALY
EUROPEAN ROBIN
UNITED KINGDOM
NIGHTINGALE
CROATIA
AMERICAN ROBIN
UNITED STATES
RED-CROWNED CRANE
CHINA
RUFOUS HORNERO
ARGENTINA
EMU
AUSTRALIA
KIWI
NEW ZEALAND

But although these wondrous places hold
a certain fascination,
the greatest nation in the world
is my own imagination!

I visit any world I wish
and never leave my chair.
There is no buddy like a book
to make me feel I'm there.

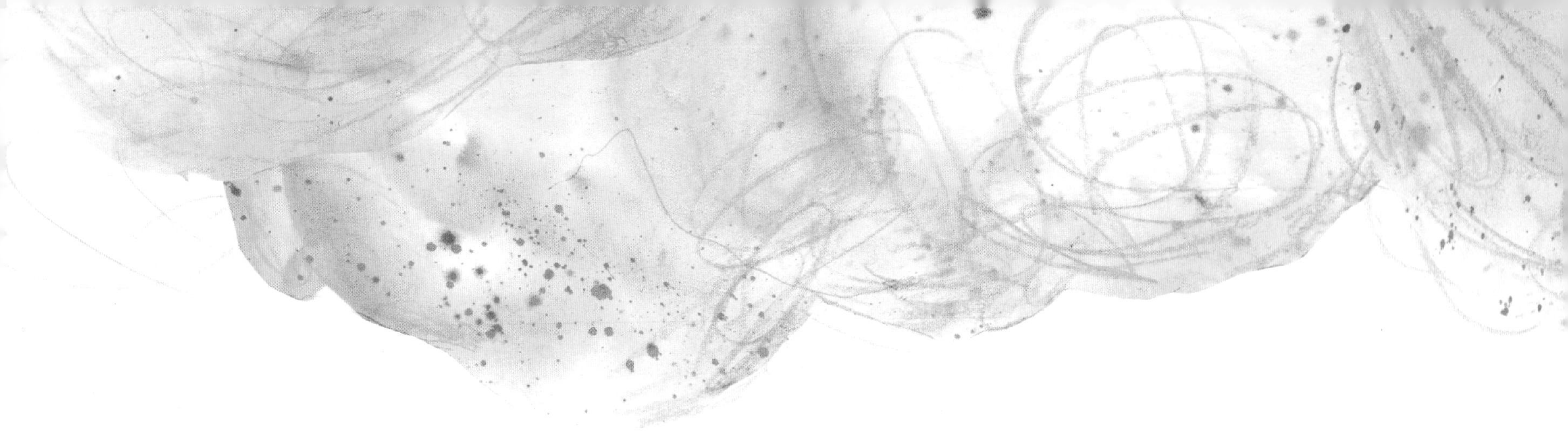

So step aboard the Book Express.
It's leaving from the station.
The only ticket needed is
your own imagination.

Whatever are you waiting for?
The adventure starts today.
Just grab a book from off the shelf ...

and you're on your way.

For Peter, Kaye, and Sarah Graham –
the best book buddies ever!
AW

To Ruth, to Dasha, to Peter, to Thyra, and, always, to Jon
BF

First published 2021 by Walker Books Ltd
87 Vauxhall Walk, London SE11 5HJ

2 4 6 8 10 9 7 5 3 1

This book has been typeset in My Happy 70s

Printed in China

British Library Cataloguing in Publication Data:
a catalogue record for this book is available
from the British Library

ISBN 978-1-4063-9604-1

www.walker.co.uk